GIRLS
A to Z

P9-DFS-394

GIRLS
A to Z

by Eve Bunting

Illustrated by Suzanne Bloom

BOYDS MILLS PRESS
AN IMPRINT OF HIGHLIGHTS
Honesdale, Pennsylvania

To all our wonderful girls:
Chris, Debbie, Tracy, Dana, Anna, Tory, and Erin
—*EB*

To my girlfriends who all work hard to help make dreams
come true.
—*SB*

Text copyright © 2002 by Eve Bunting
Illustrations copyright © 2002 by Suzanne Bloom
All rights reserved

For information about permission to reproduce selections from this book,
please contact permissions@highlights.com.

Boyds Mills Press, Inc.
An Imprint of Highlights
815 Church Street
Honesdale, Pennsylvania 18431
Printed in China
boydsmillspress.com

Publisher Cataloging-in-Publication Data (U.S.)

Bunting, Eve.
    Girls : a to z / by Eve Bunting ; illustrated by Suzanne Bloom.—1st ed.
[32] p. : col. ill. ;   cm.
Summary: Girls with names ranging from Aliki to Zoe imagine themselves in various
fun and creative professions.
ISBN: 978-1-56397-147-1 (hc) • ISBN: 978-1-62091-028-3 (pb)
1. Occupations — Juvenile literature. 2. Women — Employment — Juvenile literature.
3. Professions — Juvenile literature. (1. Occupations. 2. Women — Employment.
3. Professions. 4. Alphabet.) I. Bloom, Suzanne. II. Title.
331.7/ 02/ 082 [E] 21   CIP   HF5381.2.B86 2002
2001094574

The text of this book is set in Souvenir Medium.

10 9 8 7 6 5 4 3 2 1

Aliki is an astronaut,

Belinda likes ballet,

Chris is a computer whiz— she's online every day.

Dana is a dentist,

Eve's an engineer,

Fiona puts out fires,

Gwen's a gondolier.

Haifa likes to stay at home,

Irene makes ice cream,

Jasmine is a juggler,

Kate's a kicker for the team.

Lupe's a librarian,

Maria meditates,

Nicky is a nanny,

Olive operates.

Pat is our next president,

Quinn's the harvest queen,

Rosie races racing cars,

Sal sells gasoline.

Tanya teaches little kids
to say the alphabet,

Ula is an umpire,

Velma is a vet.

Windemere writes picture books,

Xi plays the xylophone,

Yolanda studies yoga,

Zoe's zoo's well known.

Girls,
Be anything you want to be.
Do what you want to do.
Dream any dream you want to dream.
The world is here for you.

When you grow up, what would you like to be? Here's an alphabet of possibilities.

"The sky's the limit for Bunting's assemblage of vivacious young ladies who imagine themselves in every profession under the sun. . . . A treasure that should be on every young girl's bookshelf and maybe on a boy's as well."
—*Kirkus Reviews*

"A winning alphabet book that is playful [and] inventive. [In] Bloom's exuberant portraits, . . . the children are every bit as diverse as the careers they contemplate."
—*School Library Journal*

Cover illustration copyright © 2002 by Suzanne Bloom

BOYDS MILLS PRESS
An Imprint of Highlights
815 Church Street
Honesdale, Pennsylvania 18431
boydsmillspress.com
Printed in China

$6.95

ISBN 978-1-62091-028-3

5 0 6 9 5

9 781620 910283